Hanukkah
Bear

by Eric A. Kimmel

illustrated by Mike Wohnoutka

Holiday House / New York

To Nana, who liked bears — E. A. K.

For Anna, who puts up with my growling — M. W.

The publisher thanks Rabbi Frank Tamburello for reviewing
the text and illustrations for this book.

This story first appeared in *Cricket, the Magazine for Children*,
in 1988 and as a picture book titled *The Chanukkah Guest*,
with illustrations by Giora Carmi, in 1990. This edition
has a revised text and new illustrations.

Text copyright © 2013 by Eric A. Kimmel
Illustrations copyright © 2013 by Mike Wohnoutka
All Rights Reserved
HOLIDAY HOUSE is registered in the U.S. Patent and Trademark Office.
Printed and Bound in June 2022 at Toppan Leefung, DongGuan City, China.
The artwork was created with acrylic paint.
www.holidayhouse.com
11 12 13 14 15
Library of Congress Cataloging-in-Publication Data
Kimmel, Eric A.
[Chanukkah guest]
Hanukkah bear / by Eric A. Kimmel ; illustrated by Mike Wohnoutka. — 1st ed.
p. cm.
Summary: On the first night of Hanukkah, Old Bear wanders into Bubba Brayna's house
and receives a delicious helping of potato latkes when she mistakes him for the rabbi.
Includes a recipe for latkes.
ISBN 978-0-8234-2855-7 (hardcover)
[1. Hanukkah—Fiction. 2. Bears—Fiction. 3. Old age—Fiction. 4. Jews—Fiction.]
I. Wohnoutka, Mike, ill. II. Title.
PZ7.K5648Han 2013
[E]—dc23
2012039288

ISBN 978-0-8234-3169-4 (paperback)

Old Bear awoke from his winter sleep. He poked his nose outside his den. What was that? *Mmmmmm!* Something to eat! Old Bear's empty stomach rumbled. He shook himself all over, then lumbered out of his den to follow the delicious smell.

Bubba Brayna took the last potato latke from the pan and put it in the oven with the others.

Bubba Brayna was ninety-seven years old and did not hear or see as well as she used to, but she still made the best potato latkes in the village.

Every year at Hanukkah time all her friends came to her house on the edge of the forest. How they loved those latkes! Bubba Brayna always made plenty. But tonight she made twice as many as usual. Tonight was special. Tonight the rabbi was coming.

Bubba Brayna hurried
to get ready.

Just then she heard a thump on the door.
She opened it. "Rabbi, you're here early.
How nice to see you!"
"*Grrrrumph*," growled Old Bear.
"Happy Hanukkah to you, too.
Please come in."

Old Bear walked into the house.

"I'll take your coat, Rabbi. My, how thick it is!" Bubba Brayna tugged at Old Bear's fur.

Old Bear roared. "*Grrrowwww!*"

"Oh, you want to keep your coat on? Well, that's all right. It is chilly in here."

Old Bear's nose twitched. "*Rrrrrumph!*"

"Thank you, Rabbi. How kind of you to say that. The latkes will taste even better than they smell."

Old Bear followed his nose to the oven.

"RRROOOOWRGH!"

"Rabbi, I'm surprised at you! You know we don't eat until we light the menorah."

"Grrrrr!"

"That's all right. I know you were teasing. I'll light the candles. Will you say the blessings?"

"Rrrumph."

Bubba Brayna struck a match and lit the shammes candle. Then she lit the one for the first night.

Old Bear muttered and growled. *"Rrrumph . . . grrrooooowr . . . rrrrr . . ."*

" '. . . who has kept us alive, sustained us, and enabled us to reach this season.' Oh, Rabbi, you say the blessings so beautifully!"

Bubba Brayna sat down at the table. Old Bear sat beside her. "Let's play dreidel. We'll use these nuts."

Old Bear cracked one with his teeth.

"Rabbi, you won't have any nuts for the game if you eat them."

"*Rrrrummmmr,*" growled Old Bear.

"Don't worry. I have plenty of nuts if you need more." Bubba Brayna spun the dreidel. It stopped on the letter *gimel.* "I win!" Bubba Brayna swept the nuts into her apron.

"*RRRROWRRRR!*" Old Bear roared.

"Don't be angry, Rabbi. It's only a game." She tossed him a nut. Old Bear begged for more.

"No, Rabbi, no more nuts. It's time for dinner."

Bubba Brayna opened the oven door and took out a platter piled high with steaming potato latkes. Old Bear sniffed the latkes as she set them on the table.

"Do you prefer sour cream or jam?" Bubba Brayna asked.

"Rrrughrrr!" Old Bear growled.

"Jam. I thought so." Bubba Brayna smeared five big latkes with jam and stacked them on Old Bear's plate. Old Bear gobbled them down.

Bubba Brayna laughed. "You should use a fork. You have jam all over your beard." She wet a towel and wiped Old Bear's face. "I must tell you, Rabbi. You eat like a bear."

"*GRROARRRURURRRRR!!!*"

"*I'm hungry like a bear, so I eat like one. I can see that,*" Bubba Brayna said.

Old Bear ate and ate until the latkes were gone. He felt drowsy. His head flopped on Bubba Brayna's lap. "Rabbi, you're sleepy. Who wouldn't be sleepy after such a meal? All the latkes are gone. It's time to go home."

"But before you leave, I have a Hanukkah present for you." Bubba Brayna took a red scarf from her knitting basket. She wrapped it around Old Bear's neck. "I made it myself."

"*Grrrrurrrr.*" Old Bear licked Bubba Brayna's face.

Bubba Brayna blushed. "Oh, Rabbi! At my age!"

Old Bear shuffled to the door. "*Rrrrumph,*" he growled as he walked off into the night.

"Good night to you, too, Rabbi! Happy Hanukkah!"

Bubba Brayna was washing dishes when she heard another knock. "I wonder who that is."

"Shalom, Bubba Brayna!" All her friends stood at the door wishing her a happy Hanukkah.

"Shalom, everybody!" Bubba Brayna said. "How nice to see you. I'm sorry I don't have any more latkes. The rabbi came by. He ate them all."

"Bubba Brayna, don't you recognize me?" It was the rabbi.

"The rabbi couldn't have eaten your latkes," everyone said. "He's been with us in the synagogue."

Bubba Brayna rubbed her forehead. "Something strange is happening. Rabbi, I think there is an imposter going around. He looks like you. He talks like you. He even has your beard."

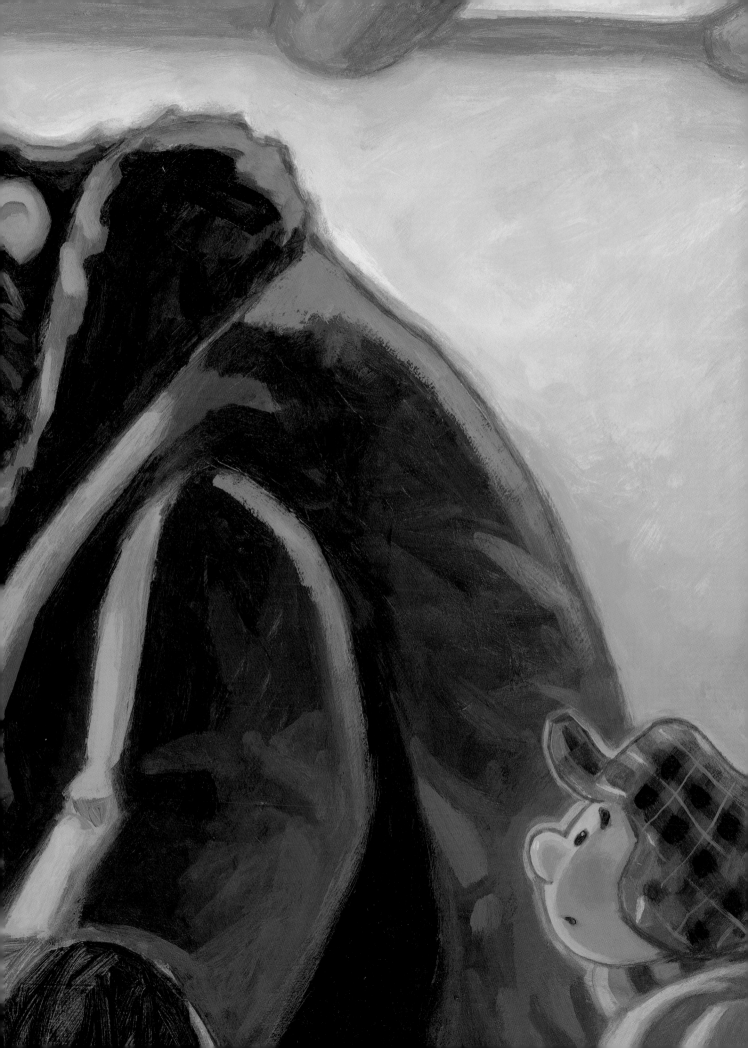

Just then the children cried, "Look at the floor! Bear
tracks!"

"A bear! And I thought it was the rabbi." Bubba Brayna
had to sit down. Soon she began to giggle. "That was a very
clever bear . . . or a very foolish Bubba Brayna. Ah well, let
the bear have a happy Hanukkah. I had a happy Hanukkah,
too. And so will you, dear friends.

"Bring some potatoes from the cellar. Fetch my grater and
bowl. Everybody has to help. You, too, Rabbi. If we all work
together, we'll soon have latkes for everyone!"

Deep in the forest Old Bear slumbered in his den. His stomach was full of potato latkes. The warm woolen scarf was wrapped snugly around his neck.

Pleasant dreams, Old Bear. And Happy Hanukkah.

Latkes

- 2 cups peeled and grated potatoes
- 1 grated onion
- 3 eggs, beaten
- 2 tablespoons matzoh meal or all-purpose flour
- 1½ teaspoons salt
- ½ cup canola or vegetable oil for frying

Directions

1. Place the potatoes in a cheesecloth and wring, extracting as much moisture as possible.

2. In a medium bowl, stir the potatoes, onion, eggs, flour, and salt together.

3. In a large heavy-bottomed skillet over medium-high heat, heat the oil until hot. Place large spoonfuls of the potato mixture into the hot oil, pressing down on them with a spatula to form ¼ to ½ inch thick patties. Brown on one side, turn and brown on the other. Let drain on paper towels. Serve hot with applesauce or sour cream.

Author's Note

Hanukkah is the Jewish Festival of Lights. The holiday commemorates a victory over the Greek army in 145 B.C.E., when the Temple in Jerusalem was restored to Jewish worship. According to tradition, there was only enough sanctified oil to light the Temple menorah for one day. The oil miraculously burned for eight days, long enough for more oil to be brought to Jerusalem.

Since then, oil and light have been part of celebrating Hanukkah. The nine-branched Hanukkah lamp—the menorah, or hanukiyah—is lit each night, beginning with one candle and ending with eight. A servant candle, the shammes, is used to light the others.

Foods cooked in oil are part of the Hanukkah celebration. Latkes (potato pancakes) and sufganiyot (jelly doughnuts) are traditional Hanukkah dishes.

Hanukkah games are played with a four-sided top called a dreidel, or sivivon. The four letters on the sides are the first letters of the Hebrew words *Nes Gadol Haya Sham*. The words mean "A Great Miracle Happened There."